This book
belongs to

_____

ON MY WAY WITH SESAME STREET™

Volume 10

Up, Down, and All Around

Featuring Jim Henson's Sesame Street Muppets

Children's Television Workshop/Funk & Wagnalls

Authors

Sandy Damashek
Andrew Gutelle
Linda Hayward
Michaela Muntean
Pat Tornborg

Illustrators

Tom Cooke
Robert Dennis
Joe Ewers
Tom Leigh
Kimberly A. McSparran
Maggie Swanson

0-8343-0084-2

1 2 3 4 5 6 7 8 9 0

A Parents' Guide to
UP, DOWN, AND ALL AROUND

Preschoolers learn much about the world around them by finding out how things relate to each other. Opposites are the easiest relationships for children to recognize: the bowl is full, the bowl is empty; Big Bird is big, Little Bird is little.

Next children come to recognize differences in degree: big, bigger, biggest. Understanding these relational concepts helps children to put their world in perspective and to communicate better: "I feel cold. Where's my warm sweater?"

"Ernie and Bert's Different Day" is a funny story about the time Ernie wanted to do everything in the opposite way. He wanted to climb up the slide and down the ladder, walk backward instead of forward, and eat cold soup instead of hot soup.

In "Follow the Leader," Ernie leads his friends over, under, and all around Sesame Street.

"What's the Biggest?" "A Big and Small Story," and "The Birthday Cake" are some activities that give children practice in recognizing opposites and relational concepts.

After reading this book, use relational concept words in your everyday conversations with your children to help them on their way to understanding this valuable preschool skill.

The Editors
SESAME STREET BOOKS

Ernie and Bert's Different Day

One morning when Bert was still **asleep** Ernie was **awake**. He had such a good idea that he couldn't wait a moment longer.

"Bert, old buddy, wake up!" Ernie said.

"Ernie! Why did you wake me up so early?" Bert yawned and rubbed his eyes.

"I have a great idea," said Ernie. "Today let's do everything in a different way! Won't that be fun, Bert?"

Bert did not think so. He liked to do the same things in the same way every day. But before Bert could answer, Ernie jumped out of bed to start his different day.

Later, Bert got up and went into the bathroom. He reached for his toothbrush, but it wasn't there.

"Ernie," called Bert, "where is my toothbrush?"

Ernie came to the door. "Where do you usually keep it?" he asked.

"**Over** the sink," said Bert.

"Today is different," said Ernie. "Today look **under** the sink for your toothbrush."

Bert sighed. Then he brushed his teeth and washed his face.

Bert went back into the bedroom. Ernie was already dressed. "Do you see anything different, Bert?" he asked.

"That's my shirt, Ernie!" said Bert.

"That's okay, Bert. You can wear mine," said Ernie.

Bert put on Ernie's shirt. "This is silly," he said. "This shirt is too **short** for me."

"Right, Bert," said Ernie. "And this shirt is too **long** for me!

"Come on. It's time for breakfast."

Ernie made toast for breakfast. He spread peanut butter on it. Then he turned the toast over and took a big bite. "Do you want a piece of upside-down toast, Bert?" he asked.

"Now you're going too far, Ernie," said Bert. He poured some Toasted Oat Yummies into a bowl. "I'll have the same breakfast that I eat every day."

Bert's bowl was **full** of Toasted Oat Yummies with milk. He carefully ate every single one.

When he was finished, the bowl was **empty**.

After breakfast, it was time to clean up. "I'll wash the dishes," said Ernie, and he ran to the sink.

"But that's my job," said Bert.

"Today is different!" said Ernie. So Ernie washed the dishes, and Bert dried each one carefully.

"You're too **fast**, Ernie," said Bert.

"You're too **slow**," said Ernie.

After the dishes were done, Ernie and Bert walked to the park. Ernie ran right up to the sprinkler.

"Ernie, don't get too **near** that sprinkler," said Bert.

"I'm staying **far** away from it."

But Ernie ran through the sprinkler.
"I'm being different, Bert!"
 "Right," said Bert.
"You're **wet**, and I'm **dry**."

Then Ernie dashed over to the sandbox and jumped in. "Look at me, Bert." "Ernie, you're being silly," said Bert. "Now you're **dirty**, and I'm still **clean**."

Ernie and Bert decided it was time to swing.

Bert pumped and pumped as hard as he could.

Ernie let his legs dangle. He hardly moved at all.

"See, Bert? I'm swinging **low**, and you're swinging **high**," said Ernie.

"Hey, Bert, I'm climbing **up** the slide," said Ernie.

"Now I'm climbing **down** the ladder."
"Ernie, that's no fun," said Bert.
"That's true, Bert," said Ernie. "But it's different!"

"Come on, Ernie!" called Bert. "It's time to go home."
"Okay, Bert," said Ernie. He followed his friend out of the playground. Bert walked **forward**, so Ernie walked **backward**.

As they walked through the park Ernie did everything differently from Bert.

When Bert took **big** steps, Ernie took **little** ones.

When Bert walked **in front of** a park bench, Ernie walked **behind** it.

When Bert walked
around a pile of leaves,
Ernie walked right
through it!

Ernie stopped to buy
some popcorn. There were
three sizes—**big**, **bigger**,
and **biggest**. Ernie
always bought the biggest
one for himself, but today was
different. So he bought the biggest cup for Bert.

"Ernie, I can't eat all of this!" said Bert, looking down at
the mountain of popcorn.

"Don't worry, Bert," said
Ernie. "I'll help you."
And he did.

"I'm very tired, Ernie," said Bert when they got home. "I'm going to relax and read the latest copy of *Pigeon News*."

Bert turned **on** the reading light next to his easy chair.

"Bert, you keep forgetting about our different day!" said Ernie. And he turned **off** the light.

"Errniee!" said Bert. "It's dark in here."

So Ernie turned the light back on.

"Now let's **open** all the windows in the apartment," he said.

"It's too windy, Ernie," said Bert. "I want the windows **closed**."

At dinner Ernie put ice cubes in his vegetable soup. "Today I will make my soup **cold**," he said.

"I like my soup **hot**, Ernie," said Bert.

After dinner, Bert put away his toys. Then he watered the plants. "I'll read you a story, Bert," said Ernie. "And they lived happily ever after," he read.

"Ernie!" cried Bert. "That's the **end** of the story, not the **beginning**."

"Right, Bert," said Ernie. "Once upon a time."

"I can't stand it anymore," said Bert. "I'm going to bed. Good night, Ernie."

"Good morning, Bert!"

A Rainy Day

Big Bird and Little Bird are getting wet.
They need some clothes to keep them dry.
Point to the things that will fit Big Bird.
Point to the things that will fit Little Bird.

Oscar's Train

"All aboard!" calls Oscar, the engineer.
Who's pulling and who's pushing?
Which train car would you like to ride on?

A Short Story
by Little Bird

If you are little,
If you are small,
If you're not big,
And not very tall,

You can fit into
Very small places,
Out-of-the-way,
Snuggly spaces.

If you are small,
It is easy to send
Your little self to
Your very best friend.

If you are little,
You can sleep anywhere—
A drawer or a slipper,
Or under a chair.

When you are little,
Traveling's easy to do.
In a pocket or backpack
You have a great view.

When you are little,
Small foods are the best—
Serve raisins and peas
To your little guest.

Though most of my friends
Are not very small,
For me being little
Is no problem at all!

What's the Biggest?

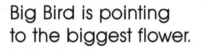

Big Bird is pointing
to the biggest flower.

Point to the biggest ball.

Point to the biggest star.

Point to the biggest fish.

MOOD FOOD

HELLO, I'M HERRY MONSTER, AND THAT MAKES ME VERY 'APPY, YA! BUT PEOPLE THINK IT IS HARD TO TELL WHEN I AM HAPPY, AND THAT MAKES ME SAD.

SAD

MAD

HAPPY

THEN PEOPLE SAY IT IS HARD TO TELL I AM SAD. THAT MAKES ME MAD! TO SHOW PEOPLE HOW I AM FEELING, I MAKE A SALAD. YOU, TOO, CAN SHOW PEOPLE HOW YOU ARE FEELING BY MAKING A SALAD.

Mood Food

Note: Adult supervision is suggested.

What you need:

For the face: lettuce; red cabbage; slices of cheese or meat

For the eyes: hard-boiled eggs, sliced lengthwise or across; sliced green or black olives

For the mouth: slices of melon or half of a banana, curved upward or downward; a pineapple ring (for a surprised mouth); a strawberry cut in half

For the ears: a pear cut in quarters lengthwise

For the nose and cheeks: cherries, berries, or cherry tomatoes, cut in half

For the hair: shredded carrots, cole slaw, bean or alfalfa sprouts

What you do:

Just place the ingredients of your choice together to make a face that shows your mood.

A Big and Small Story

Herry Monster's coat is too small.
Bert's coat is too big.
Betty Lou's coat is just right.

Now Herry's coat is just right.
But Bert's coat is too small.
And Betty Lou's coat is too big.

At last everyone's coat
is just the right size.

But what about the hats?

The Birthday Cake

Tomorrow is Bert's birthday. I will make him a little cake in this little pan. I will ask Little Bird to come to a little birthday party for Bert.

Point to the little pan.

But if I make a *bigger* cake in this *bigger* pan, I can ask Little Bird and Big Bird to come to a bigger birthday party for Bert.

Point to the bigger pan.

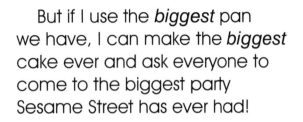

But if I use the *biggest* pan we have, I can make the *biggest* cake ever and ask everyone to come to the biggest party Sesame Street has ever had!

Point to the biggest pan.

Gee, Bert is in for a big surprise!

Point to the big mess.

Follow the Leader

"Hey, Bert, let's play follow the leader," said Ernie as he ran down the steps of 123 Sesame Street.

Bert shook his head. "Not now, Ernie," he said. "I'm on my way to the library. I don't have time to play a game."

"Gee, Bert," said Ernie, "I know a shortcut to the library. If you follow me, you'll get there in no time!"

in front of

Ernie and Bert met Grover **in front of** Hooper's Store.

behind

"Where are you going?" asked Grover.

"We're going to the library," answered Bert.

"Do you want to come with us, Grover? Just walk **behind** Bert," said Ernie.

over

"**Over** we go!" said Ernie as he jumped **over** a fire hydrant.

"**Over** we go," said Bert and Grover. They jumped **over** a fire hydrant, too.

under

"Now let's go **under** here," called Ernie. He crawled **under** a big bush next to the sidewalk.

"Ernie, are you sure you know where you are going?" asked Bert.

"Just follow me, Bert," said Ernie. "This is my shortcut."

in

BAKERY

They walked down another street. Suddenly Ernie stopped. "Hmm. Here's the bakery. Let's go **in**," he said. So the three went **in**.

out

BAKERY

Four came **out**. "How did you know where to find me?" asked Cookie Monster.

between

Next Ernie and Bert and Grover and Cookie Monster walked **between** two houses...

across

...and cut **across** a back yard.

Then Ernie led the gang into the playground. Big Bird was waiting for them.

"Hello, everybody!" he said. "I've been watching you. You jumped over a fire hydrant, crawled under a bush, went into the bakery and out of the bakery, and walked between two houses and across a back yard. Are you playing follow the leader?"

"No," said Bert. "We're going to the library."

"Well," said Ernie, "we're going to the library–and we're playing follow the leader, too. Do you want to play?"

top

Bert and Grover and
Cookie Monster and Big Bird
followed Ernie to the **top**
of the jungle gym.

bottom

"Let's try the slide next,"
Ernie said.
So they all slid to the
bottom of the slide.

near

Then they stopped to rest **near** a boat pond.

"Ernie," said Bert, as soon as he had caught his breath, "when are we going to get to the library?"

far

"It won't be long now," said Ernie. "Look."

Far away, they could see a busy city street.

"Follow me, everybody," said Ernie.

"Well, Bert, here we are!" said Ernie.

"Oh, neato! The library. Okay, everybody, follow me!" said Bert.

So Bert and Grover and Cookie Monster and Big Bird and Ernie climbed up the steps to the library.

"Hey, Bert. Wait until you see the shortcut I have for the way home!" called Ernie.